Grand Scam
A FILM BY MATT REHER & DREW FALCHETTA

What will we see? Your call.
The Grand Scam. It looks neat!
The Grand Scam
Vin

PUP CAMP
THE TWINS WIN
THE GRAND SCAM
THE BAT
the BAT
TICKETS

The Twins Win
How about The Twins Win?

No. Let's go to The Grand Scam. It's a big hit.
Scam

I want to see *The Twins Win*. Or we could see *The Bat*.
Sam and I want to see *The Grand Scam*. Please, Dan?

OK. I'm in. The Grand Scam it is.
Thank you, Dan! You stand here. I'll get the tickets. My treat.
TICK

One for Dan.
One for Sam.
One for me.

CONCESSIONS
You go in and get seats. I'll get a big treat for us to split.

One big cup, please. Fill it up!
BIG CUP
MED BAG
SM BAG
KIDS BAG
POPC
Candy

Let's sit by the wall.
I can't see over that tall man and his hat.

These seats are the pits.

These look good. They look brand new.

Dan! Matt! I can't see you. Put your hands up! Stand up!
PO
CO

Shh! Don't shout. We're over here!
POP
COR

Rats! We should have seen The Twins Win.
POP